Winter Wheat

BRENDA Z. GUIBERSON

Winter Wheat

ILLUSTRATED BY MEGAN LLOYD

HENRY HOLT AND COMPANY · NEW YORK

For the ancient rolling hills where
the Wolf Fork cuts through the Blues
—B. Z. G.

To Laura Godwin
Thanks for sending me to the "four corners"
—M. L. L.

Henry Holt and Company, Inc. / *Publishers since 1866*
115 West 18th Street / New York, New York 10011

Henry Holt is a registered trademark of Henry Holt and Company, Inc.
Text copyright © 1995 by Brenda Z. Guiberson
Illustrations copyright © 1995 by Megan Lloyd. All rights reserved.
Published in Canada by Fitzhenry & Whiteside Ltd.,
195 Allstate Parkway, Markham, Ontario L3R 4T8.
Library of Congress Cataloging-in-Publication Data
Guiberson, Brenda Z. Winter wheat / Brenda Z. Guiberson; illustrated by Megan Lloyd.
1. Winter wheat—Juvenile literature.   2. Farm life—Juvenile literature.   [1. Farm life.   2. Wheat.]
I. Lloyd, Megan, ill.   II. Title.   SB119.W5G85   1994   633.1'1—dc20   93-41365
ISBN 0-8050-1582-5 / First Edition—1995
Printed in the United States of America on acid-free paper. ∞

1   3   5   7   9   10   8   6   4   2

The artist used watercolors on Twin Rocker handmade paper to create the paintings for this book.

One day in late August a farmer, Albert, starts up the Caterpillar tractor. His dog, Stitch, jumps up from the front porch and barks at the noisy machine. Tulip, the cow, kicks out her hind leg and moos. The early-morning sun glistens off a shiny glass headlamp as the old engine coughs and rattles while it warms up.

Albert is off to work. He drives around the fence and past the aspens. The smell of oil is strong as the tractor struggles up the road to the steep hills below the pine forest. This is where he plants the wheat—strong, hardy kernels that live through the winter. Tulip stays in the corral, but Stitch follows the tractor up the narrow dirt road, sniffing for pheasant and coyote.

For the whole long day, and several days after, the farmer hitches a plow behind the tractor and pulls it through the fields. Albert bounces in his seat as the tractor tilts and strains over the steep slopes. The plow turns over weeds and old wheat stubble, leaving thick brown clumps of dirt. The summer days are hot and dry and the tractor kicks up a cloud of dust. Stitch stays away from the noise and chases a magpie through the shady pines.

Albert leaves the plow at the edge of the field and hitches up the
harrow. He will use the harrow to break up the heavy clusters of dirt.
For several more days he drives the same curves again. The clumps
of soil crumble into small, even pieces. The fields look fresh and
smooth, like ribbons across the hills. But Albert is sunburned and
sweaty and covered with dust. Stitch has twigs and stickers in her
fur from head to tail.

The ground is too dry for planting, so Albert works near the house. One day he picks warm, juicy tomatoes and hangs oregano to dry in the shed. Another day he climbs the orchard ladder to fill his pail with apples. Stitch jumps at an apple that falls to the ground and she takes a crunchy bite.

Then one morning Albert wakes to the fresh, damp smell of rain. "This is it," he says. "The dirt is good and wet. Now I can plant my wheat." He empties bags of seeds into the seed drill, which will drop the kernels into straight rows in the ground. For the next several days he and Stitch are back in the fields. The tractor moves slowly over the mushy hills as seeds and fertilizer fall behind the tractor. The farmer plants every slope and valley, working late into the setting sun. He honks as he comes around the last curve. Stitch is asleep halfway down the narrow road.

The aspen leaves turn a shimmering yellow in the fall. The farmer cleans out the chicken coop and digs potatoes and onions to store in the root cellar. During a rainy week, he works inside on a new shelf for the kitchen. Stitch puts her nose into the sawdust and spreads it all over, but Albert does not notice. He is excited about what he sees out the window. The wheat has sprouted, and all the brown hillsides have turned bright green. "Just look at that," he says. "Best shade of green I ever saw."

In the next few weeks, the days turn cool and crisp. Albert gets out the apple press and sells cider and pumpkins by the barn. Stitch barks and runs over to the narrow dirt road. The farmer looks up to see a flock of noisy geese flap down into the green fields. Two deer that have jumped over the barbed wire fence are in the fields too. All of them are nibbling at the tender shoots of wheat. Albert pats the dog on the head and watches. "I see them, Stitch," he says. "I guess we can share a little with our friends."

Soon the valley is covered in snow. Albert brings hay down from the barn loft for Tulip and pours warm gravy over Stitch's dinner. When neighbors stop by, he dishes up berry cobbler and cream. Everyone is happy about the snowfall. It is a thick white blanket that will protect the young wheat over the winter.

At the end of January, it snows almost every day. The farmer keeps a
path shoveled to the barn and checks on Tulip and the chickens. One
frosty afternoon Stitch barks and barks from the front porch. Albert
comes out with his hat and gloves. A herd of elk have come down
from the snowy mountains and knocked over the fence. They make
long shadows across the slopes as they eat the wheat. The farmer
counts them. Five on the north slope. A dozen on the crest of the
hill. At least twenty on the south side. "Oh bother, Stitch," he says.
"We have work to do."

Albert calls the neighbors and gets his truck warmed up. Three farmers and a dog crowd the front seat for a ride to the hills. Stitch barks and jumps across the crusty snow as they chase the elk back into the woods. "Can't do a thing about this trampled wheat," says Albert. "But I am going to fix the fence."

The snow is gone by springtime. Albert sips his morning coffee in the orchard where he can smell the blossoms. He puts tall stakes in the garden and plants a crop of sugar peas. Then he and Stitch walk up the spongy hillside to check the wheat. A few geese nibble at the long green stalks.

Everything is growing nicely in the warmth, including the weeds. On the west slope, the farmer finds thistle choking the stalks. He cannot plow over the weeds because the grain is too tall. "We lost wheat to the elk," he says. "Now some is lost to the weeds. I sure hope we don't lose much to the weather."

Summer is hot and sunny with a few good days of rain. While Albert is busy with peaches and cherries, the wheat grows three feet tall. The stalks flower, go to seed, and dry out in the heat. From the top of the orchard ladder, the farmer watches the wheat fields turn golden yellow. Late one afternoon, Albert and Stitch stir up grasshoppers as they walk over the hill. At the top, a gust of warm wind sends a ripple through the dry fields. "We better get those combines here right away," says Albert. "This crop is ready for harvest."

Two gigantic combines arrive at dawn. They come to cut the wheat stalks and separate the grain from the rest of the plant. Albert takes down a section of fence to let them through. Stitch and Tulip run into the barn when the machines swing around the corner. In low gear, the heavy combines crawl up the steep hill. They bend and groan at every turn and reach out beyond the edges of the road. Dirt and pebbles crumble beneath them as they pass.

At the top, the combines roll onto the fields with their front reels turning. The early morning is already blistering hot. The combines move at less than two miles per hour, but they are so huge that they quickly mow down the crop. Wheat kernels collect inside the machines. At the back, the combines spit out leftover straw and chaff. Everywhere, there is dust, dust, dust in the air.

Albert is ready with the truck for the first load of grain. Stitch sits on the front seat with her nose out the window. Golden seeds pour from the chute and fill the back of the truck. The scratchy wheat chaff in the air makes the farmer itch all over. Stitch sneezes. Albert sneezes. Both noses stuff up with dust. The neighbor, looking cool and comfortable, waves from the air-conditioned cab of his shiny machine.

Albert and Stitch take the heavy load to a grain elevator near town. A woman in a plaid shirt walks out to check the wheat. Stitch sniffs at her clipboard. "Well, here come a couple of good farmers," she says. "Plumpest, driest kernels I've seen all week." Albert smiles at the report and watches the wheat as it's loaded into the metal building. Soon it will be sold to a flour company far away.

When the harvest is done, the combines move up the valley to other fields. Albert and Stitch spend a long, quiet morning on the porch listening to the hum of bees in the garden. But soon the tractor is moving again. The farmer pulls the rake across the hills to collect the straw that the combines have left behind. He uses the truck to bring back a huge load of straw. It is stored in the barn to make clean bedding for Tulip and the chickens.

Now the farmer takes a close look at the tractor. He puts in clean oil and new plugs and changes the filters. He checks and greases all the moving parts. With the garden hose, he washes off layers of dirt and grime. Finally, he polishes the tractor seat and shines up the glass on the headlamps. Stitch runs over to the narrow dirt road and barks. They are ready to start again. It is another day in late August and time to plow the fields for a new crop of winter wheat.

Winter Wheat Can Be for the Birds

People have been eating wheat for thousands of years and have thought about the best ways to grow it. They have developed soft white varieties for pastry flour and hard red grains to make bread. Durum wheat is the kind that is made into pasta.

Some wheat is planted in the spring, harvested in late summer, and is called *spring wheat*. Other varieties are planted in the fall. They need a period of cold winter weather to signal the crop to an early growth spurt in the spring. This type of wheat is called *winter wheat*.

Many farmers have discovered that the cycle of growth for winter wheat has definite advantages over growing spring wheat. Winter wheat makes better use of the moisture available in the fall and spring and yields about twenty percent more grain. Its roots are well established by springtime, which helps to hold down the soil and choke out weeds. The crop is ready for harvest weeks before spring wheat, reducing the possibility for damage by disease or the weather.

Even more important, during these times of disappearing wetlands and loss of wildlife habitat, the winter wheat cycle allows the farmer and wildlife to share the same piece of land. Migrating ducks and geese can graze on green stalks of winter wheat without affecting the amount of grain that will be harvested in the summer. Birds looking for nesting places can use a field of winter wheat in the spring because the grass will be tall enough for good cover, and the fields will not be disturbed by farm machinery as fields with many spring crops will be. Further, winter wheat can sometimes be planted right into the stubble on the ground left from the harvest. This process, called zero-tillage, helps to reduce erosion, keeps more moisture in the soil, and is less disruptive to wildlife. Organizations dedicated to the conservation of wildlife help interested farmers explore methods of growing winter wheat that also restore eating and nesting places to our migrating birds.